THE USBORNE
# FIRST BOOK OF THE
# RECORDER

Caroline Hooper and Philip Hawthorn

Designed by Jan McCafferty

Illustrated by Simone Abel

Original music and arrangements by
Caroline Hooper and Philip Hawthorn

Series editor: Jane Chisholm

# About this book

There are lots of different types of recorders. This book is all about the most common type, called the soprano recorder.

At the end of the book you can find out about some other types of recorders.

## Reading music

You can find out how to read music so you can play tunes on your recorder.

You can also find out how music is written down.

## Learning to play

You can learn how to play different musical sounds, called notes.

Each time you learn a new note, the page has a red corner with the note's name on it.

This helps you to look the notes up quickly and easily.

Sometimes there are high and low versions of the same note.

For example, C' is a higher version of the note C.

## Words and symbols

Musical words and symbols are explained simply and clearly as they appear in the book.

Find out what this means on page 30.

How many beats are there?

Find out what this means on page 22.

Throughout the book there are puzzles to help you learn.

legato

## Recorder facts

There are some amazing stories and facts about the recorder. For instance, you can find out what King Henry VIII of England has to do with recorder music.

You can find out about the biggest recorders in the world...

...and the smallest recorders in the world.

There are also some tunes you can play with a friend.

# About your recorder

Recorders are made of wood or plastic. Most have two or three sections, which fit together. Here you can find out what each part is called and how to fit them together.

This is the middle joint.

This is the foot joint.

On some recorders this section is attached to the middle joint.

## Taking your recorder apart ...

## ... and putting it together again.

If the joints are stiff, you can buy special grease to rub on them.

Hold the head joint firmly in one hand and the middle joint in the other. Gently twist the joints as you pull them apart.

Some recorders are in three sections. If your recorder has three parts, remove the foot joint in the same way.

Push the head joint onto the top of the middle joint. Then line up the holes with the hole in the mouthpiece.

If your recorder has three parts, set the holes on the foot joint so they are a little to the right of the other holes.

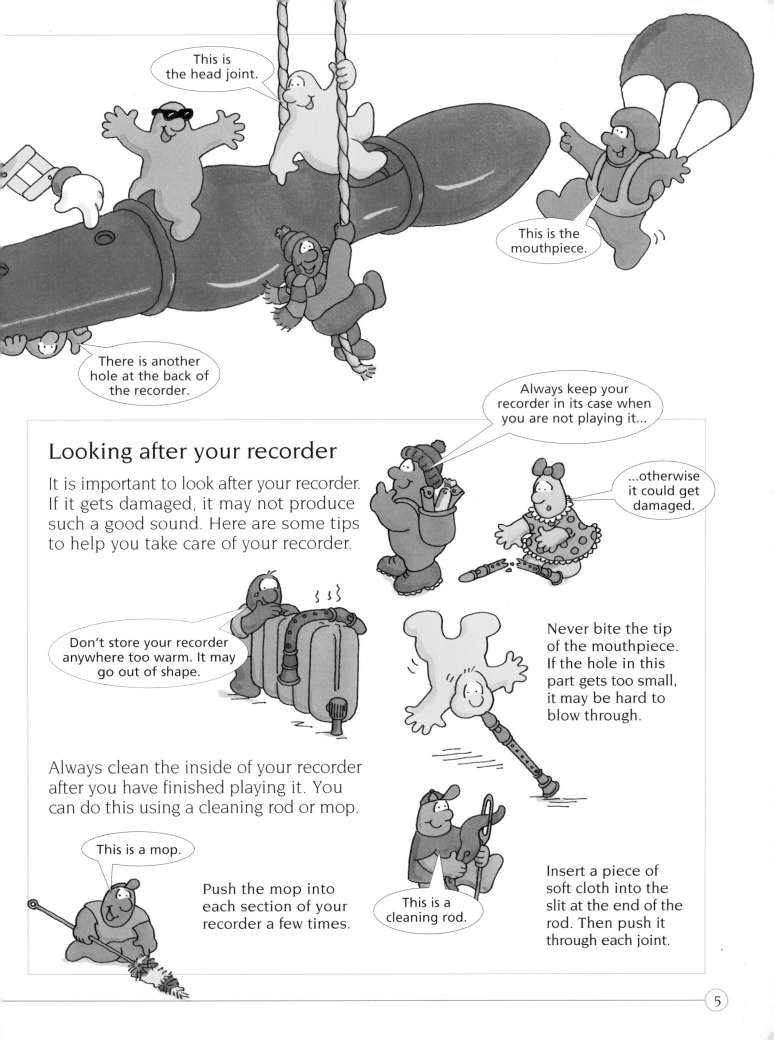

## Looking after your recorder

It is important to look after your recorder. If it gets damaged, it may not produce such a good sound. Here are some tips to help you take care of your recorder.

Always clean the inside of your recorder after you have finished playing it. You can do this using a cleaning rod or mop.

Push the mop into each section of your recorder a few times.

Never bite the tip of the mouthpiece. If the hole in this part gets too small, it may be hard to blow through.

Insert a piece of soft cloth into the slit at the end of the rod. Then push it through each joint.

# How to hold your recorder

You can sit or stand to play the recorder. Whichever you choose, always make sure your hands and fingers are relaxed, and try not to hunch your shoulders.

Prop your music up at eye level.

Hold your elbows out a little.

Hold your recorder pointing slightly away from your body.

Keep your head up and your back straight.

If you have to bend down to read it, the sound might not be clear when you play.

## Where to put your fingers

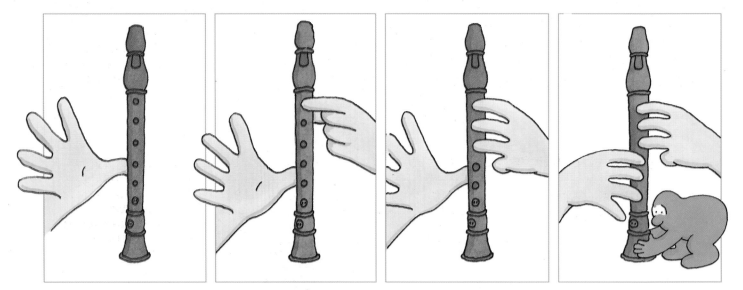

Place your right thumb on the back of the recorder between the fourth and fifth holes to hold it steady.

Then cover the hole on the back with your left thumb, and cover the first hole on the front with your first finger.

Now try covering the next two holes on your recorder with the second and third fingers of your left hand.

Cover the other holes with your right-hand fingers. Use your little finger to cover the holes on the foot joint.

# Making a sound

When you first try to blow, cover only the thumb hole and the first hole, using your right thumb to support the recorder. Put your lips around the tip of the mouthpiece, just far enough to feel comfortable. Then take a deep breath and blow very gently. When you are blowing, try to keep the flow of air as steady as you can.

Don't blow too hard or it will make your recorder squeak.

If you don't blow hard enough, or you run out of breath, it will sound like a vacuum cleaner being turned off.

Sometimes the air passage gets blocked with moisture from your breath.

If this happens, put your finger across the hole in the mouthpiece and blow sharply.

## Useful tip

Make sure your fingers are completely covering the holes. You can check to see if you are doing it correctly by pressing your fingers down hard, then removing them. You should be able to see full circle marks on your fingers.

The circles should be in the center of each finger...

...and slightly to one side on your thumb.

# Using your tongue when you blow

To make a clear sound, say "ta" very gently as you blow. This is called tonguing. It makes the sound very crisp and clear.

Try saying "ta-ta-ta" as you blow. Make each sound as even as you can.

# All about musical notes

Music is made up of lots of sounds called notes. These are named after the first seven letters of the alphabet.

## What are notes like?

Some notes are high and others are low. You can change from one note to another by covering different holes.

A note lasts for as long as you blow.

## Playing your first note

When you learned how to make a sound on page 7, you covered the thumb hole and the first hole. This note is called B.

The picture on the right shows you which holes to cover to play B.

Cover this hole with your left thumb.

Cover this hole with the first finger of your left hand.

B

Every time you learn a new note, there will be a picture like this, to show you where to put your fingers.

Make sure these two holes are completely covered.

Keep your other fingers above their holes.

Be careful not to cover any other holes by mistake.

# Writing notes down

Music is written on a set of five lines called a staff. Each note has its own place on the staff. Some go on the lines and others in the spaces.

The sign at the beginning of the staff is called a treble clef.

# Playing a rhythm

A rhythm is made up of a series of beats. The ticking of a clock and the beating of your heart are both rhythms.

Say the words on the right. Try to make each word last the same length of time.

Now say the words in your head. Play a B on your recorder for each word.

# Music symbols

There are symbols in music that tell you how many beats to count for each note you play. A note which lasts for one beat is called a quarter note.

This is a quarter note. It lasts for one beat.

## Another rhythm to clap

Say the words below, making each quarter note the same length. The longer words are split into two parts. Count one beat for each part.

Clap your hands as you say the words. There are three claps on the first line and four on the second.

| Left, | right, | left | |
|-------|--------|------|---|
| (clap) | (clap) | (clap) | |
| Sol | diers | mar | ching |
| (clap) | (clap) | (clap) | (clap) |

The second time you say the word "left" it lasts for two beats.

It is like saying "le-eft".

| Left, | | right, | left | |
|-------|---|--------|------|---|
| (clap) | | (clap) | (clap) | (silent clap) |
| Sol | - | diers | mar | - ching |
| (clap) | | (clap) | (clap) | (clap) |

The rhythm might sound better if both lines have the same number of beats. You can make the top line four beats long by giving the word at the end two beats.

Clap once as you say the word "left", then count the extra beat in your head.

# Two-beat notes

A note which lasts for two beats is called a half note. It looks like a white quarter note

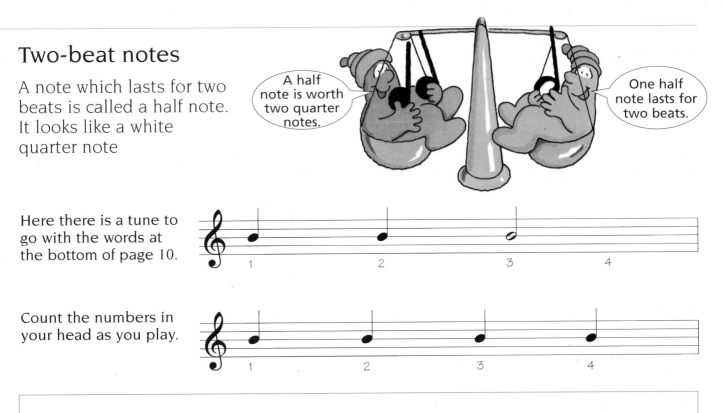

Here there is a tune to go with the words at the bottom of page 10.

Count the numbers in your head as you play.

# Dividing up the music

Music is divided up into sections called measures. Each measure contains the same number of beats. The numbers after the first treble clef tell you how many beats are in each measure. These numbers are called the time signature.

# A tune with half notes

Here is a tune to play. Clap the rhythm first, then play the tune on your recorder.

Count two beats for each half note.

# Some more notes

On these two pages you can find out about the note A. You can also learn about notes which last for four beats.

## Playing the note A

Put your fingers on the recorder as if you are going to play a B. Then put your left-hand middle finger on the second hole. This note is A.

The note A is written in the space just below the B line.

A sounds lower than B, so it is lower down on the staff.

A

In the picture on the left, the black dots show you which holes to cover.

Listen to the notes A and B.

Can you hear the difference between the two notes.

It might help to say the words in your head as you play the notes.

Old    B    New    A

## Four-beat notes

A note which lasts for four beats is called a whole note. It looks like a half note without a stick. There is a whole note at the end of this tune.

A whole note is worth four quarter beats.

How many half notes is a whole note worth?

Find out the answer on page 63.

A    whole    note,    in    this    song

It's    ve - ry    long.

# Leaving gaps in music

Sometimes there are gaps in music when no sound is made. These are called rests. There are symbols to tell you how long each rest lasts.

When you see a rest, count the number of beats in your head.

| Note symbol | Rest symbol | Length in beats |
|---|---|---|
| Quarter note | 𝄽 | 1 |
| Half note | ▬ | 2 |
| Whole note | ▬ | 4 |

A half rest only lasts for two beats.

Imagine it as a weak rest which has to sit on the line.

A whole rest hangs from the line.

Imagine it as a strong rest which can hang on for four beats.

## Rest game

This game will help you to practice using rests. Say these words and clap the rhythm.

Ice cold cream cakes

When you get to the rest, say "rest" silently in your head, and don't clap.

Ice cold cream (rest)

Now replace the second quarter note with a rest too.

Ice (rest) cream (rest)

## A tune with rests

The music below has rests in it. Say the words, clap the rhythm, then play the tune.

This is a quarter rest.

Remember to leave a gap of one beat.

### Hopscotch

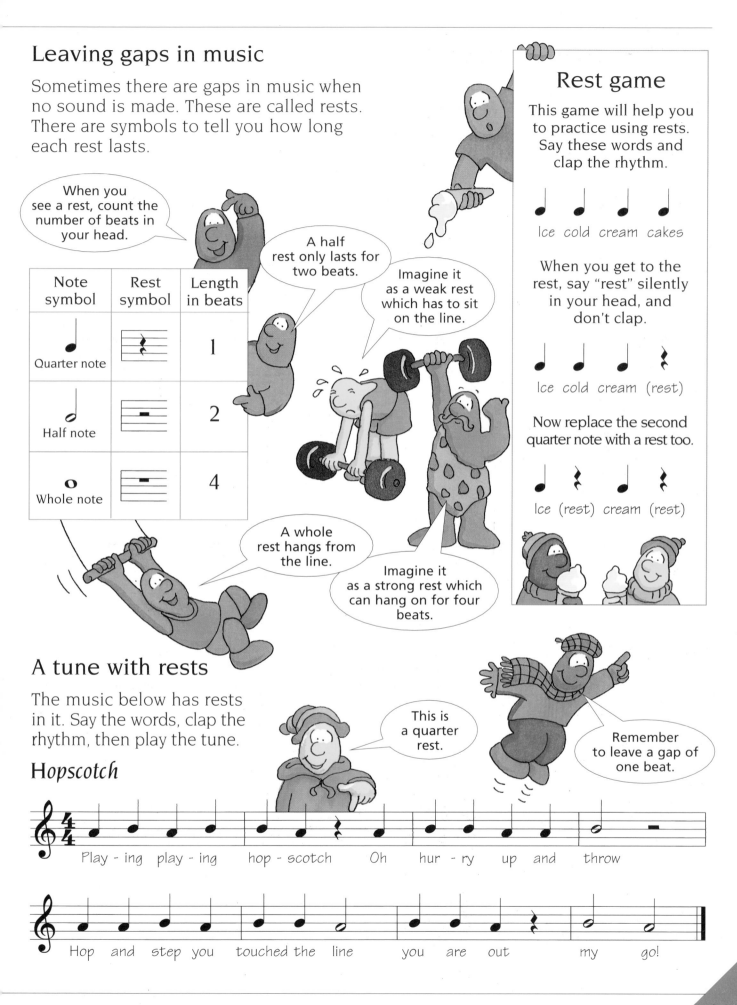

Play - ing play - ing    hop - scotch    Oh    hur - ry    up    and    throw

Hop    and    step    you    touched    the    line    you    are    out    my    go!

# Taking breaths

When you play your recorder, it is important to breathe in the right places so you don't interrupt the flow of the music.

When you take a breath, don't take the recorder out of your mouth.

Make sure you don't blow too hard after you have taken a breath.

## Playing G

Put your fingers on the recorder as if you are going to play A. Then put the third finger of your left hand on the next hole.

Notice that, as notes on the staff go up and down, so do the sounds.

# Dotted notes

A dot after a note makes it half as long again. So a dotted half note lasts for three quarter beats.

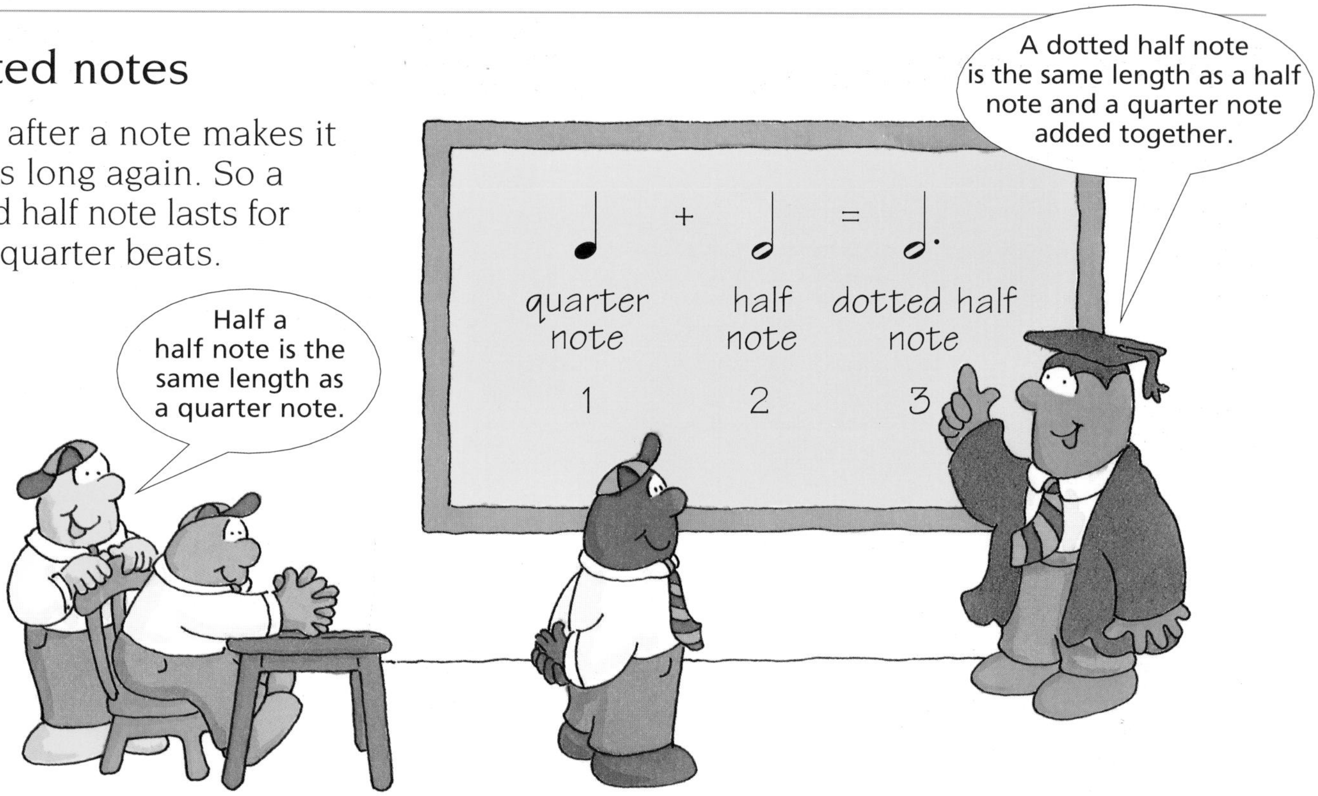

> A dotted half note is the same length as a half note and a quarter note added together.

> Half a half note is the same length as a quarter note.

quarter note    +    half note    =    dotted half note

1      2      3

# A new time signature

A number three on the top means there are three beats in each measure. A number four on the bottom tells you they are quarter beats.

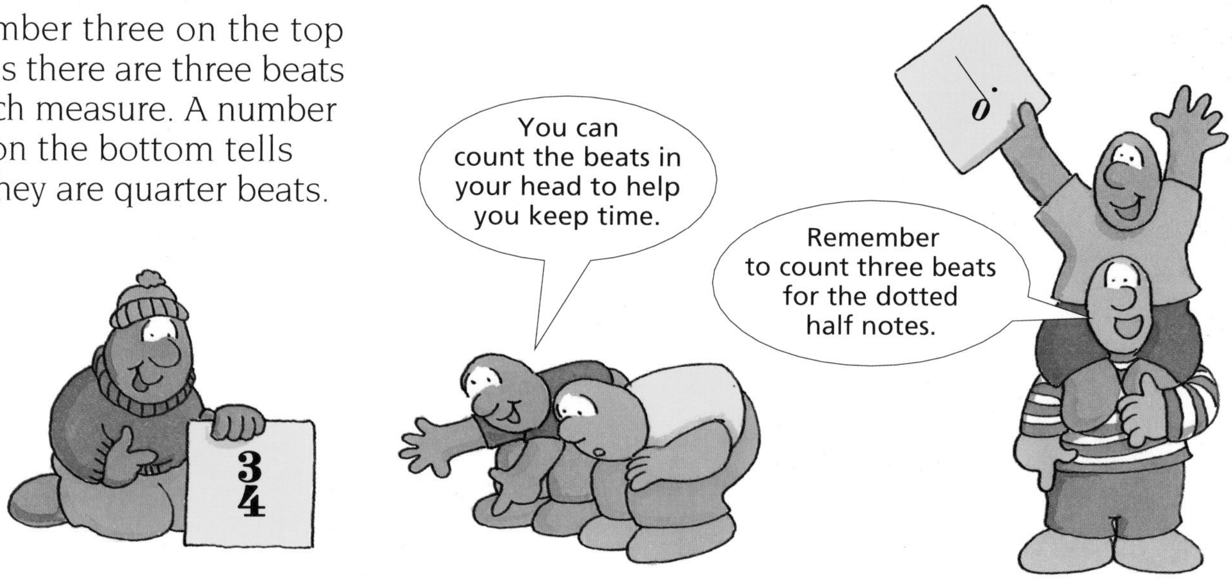

> You can count the beats in your head to help you keep time.

> Remember to count three beats for the dotted half notes.

$\frac{3}{4}$

## Cuckoo song

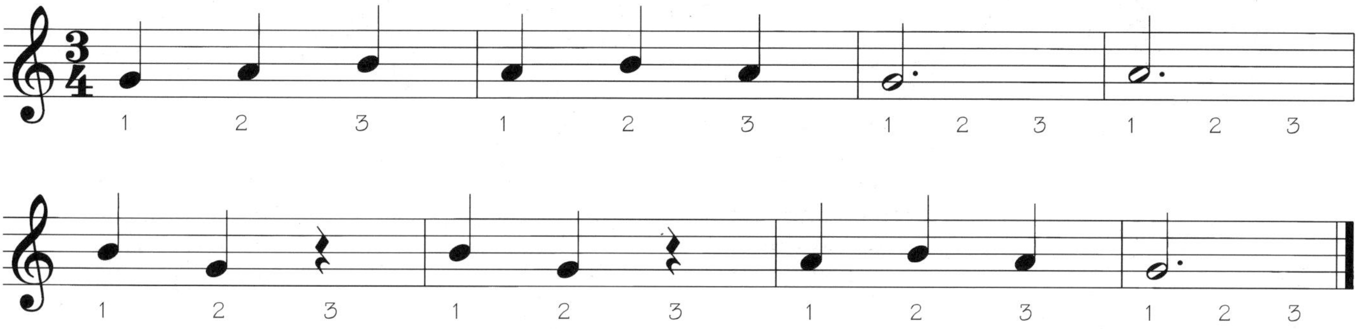

# Shorter notes

So far, you have played notes which last for one, two, three or four beats. There is also a shorter note, called an eighth note. An eighth note lasts for half a quarter beat.

This is an eighth note.

It looks like a quarter note with a tail.

Two eighth notes are the same length as one quarter note

This is an eighth rest.

It tells you to leave a gap of half a beat before playing the next note.

When two or more eighth notes are written next to each other, their tails are often joined together.

## Rhythms with eighth notes

See if you can clap the rhythms on the right. It will help to say the words as you clap.

Once in a blue moon

Lav-en-ders blue dil-ly dil-ly  lav-en-ders  green

Fred-die had a fright in the mid-dle of the night

## Playing E

Put your fingers on your recorder as if you are going to play G. Then cover the next two holes with the first two fingers of your right hand.

Blow very gently.

Remember to use your tongue for each note.

Lower notes do not need as much breath as higher ones.

E is written on the bottom line of the staff. Practice playing G and E.

Make sure you move both fingers at the same time.

E

# A tune with eighth notes

The numbers under the notes will help you count the beats. When you count two eighth notes, say "and" for the second one.

*In the tune below there are four eighth notes joined together.*

## Tribal dance

# Starting with part of a measure

Some tunes start with part of a measure. This is often called an upbeat. Where there is an upbeat, the beats in the first and last measures add up to one measure.

*The upbeat lasts for one beat, so you need to count three beats before you start.*

*It may help to count the missing beats in your head before starting to play.*

# Amazing recorder fact

*This must have been the first rock music!*

*The first recorder was made from a piece of bone.*

The earliest recorder ever found was made between 25,000 and 22,000 BC. At this time many people lived in caves.

E

# Tying notes together

Sometimes two or more notes on the same line or space are joined together with a curved line. These are called tied notes.

When two notes are tied, play the first note for as long as both notes added together.

Play this note for four beats.

Don't play a new note here.

This is a tie.

Tied notes are always on the same line or space.

## Count the beats

On the right there are some tied notes. See if you can figure out how many beats to count.

This lasts for three beats.

This lasts for four beats.

How many beats do you count for these two sets of notes?

Find out the answers on page 63.

## Playing D

Place your fingers on your recorder as if you are going to play E. Now put the third finger of your right hand over the first double hole.

Make sure you cover both small holes.

D

The note D is written just underneath the bottom line of the staff.

Practice the measures above to help you get used to the fingering.

# Dotted quarter notes

Remember, a dot after a note makes it half as long again. So a dotted quarter note lasts for one and a half beats.

## Tunes to play

Play the tunes below. Remember to watch out for the tied notes and the dotted notes.

### English folk song

### Merrily we roll along

# Repeating music

Sometimes there are symbols which tell you to play some or all of the music again. These are called repeat marks.

## Music with two repeat marks

When you see two repeat marks in a tune, play everything between them again.

Play measures one and two. Then play measures three and four twice. Then play measures five and six.

## Repeating from the beginning

Sometimes a tune only has the second type of repeat mark (the one with the dots on the left). This tells you to go back to the beginning and play all the music before the sign again.

Ignore the repeat sign the second time you reach it, and play the rest of the tune.

# Repeat marks game

Here are some measures with repeat marks. Each measure has a number instead of notes. Can you figure out the order of the measures?

Find out the answers on page 63.

# Playing high C

Put your fingers on the recorder as if you are going to play A. Now, lift your first finger, leaving your thumb and middle finger in place.

C'

C' is written in the third space up on the staff.

The note B can have its stick pointing up or down.

Notes above the middle line have their sticks pointing down.

C B C A

B G C

Keep your other fingers ready to cover their holes.

To keep your recorder steady, support it with your right thumb.

# First and second endings

Sometimes a repeated section has two different endings. The first time through, play the measure marked "1". The second time, skip this, and play the measure marked "2".

Play this measure the first time through.

Play this measure the second time through.

# In-between notes

In between the notes named after the letters of the alphabet there are extra notes called sharps and flats. On this page you can find out about sharp notes.

## Sharps

A sharp note is slightly higher than the note it takes its name from, but slightly lower than the next note up.

This is a sharp sign.

The sign is written after the letter...

...so F sharp is written F#.

F sharp is slightly higher than F, and slightly lower than G.

## Playing F sharp

Hold your recorder as if you are going to play E. Now lift the first finger of your right hand and put down your third finger.

The sharp sign is written before the note on the staff.

F sharp is written in the first space up on the staff.

It has a sharp sign in front of it so you know it is not an ordinary F.

F#

You can find out more about the note F on page 34.

A sharp sign also affects any notes with the same name which come after it in the measure.

So this note is F sharp, too.

Play the measures above slowly at first. You can gradually speed them up when you have played them a few times.

# A new time signature

Some tunes have a time signature called 6/8. The six means there are six beats in each measure. The eight tells you they are eighth beats.

In 6/8 time, you can either count in eighth beats, or in dotted quarter beats, with two dotted quarter beats in each measure.

*Say the words under these two sets of eighth notes.*

*They have a slightly different rhythm.*

In 3/4 time the eighth notes are divided into three sets of two, giving the rhythm three strong beats.

*In the month of Ap- ril*

*Si - lent - ly    si - lent - ly*

In 6/8 time the eighth notes are divided into two groups of three, so there are two strong beats.

## Tunes in 6/8 time

The numbers under the staff will help you to get the rhythm right.

*Watch out for the F sharps.*

*Remember, this is an F sharp, too.*

### Fairground ride

1 2 3 4 5 6    1 2 3 4 5 6    1 2 3 4 5 6    1 2 3 4 5 6

### Drink to me only with thine eyes

1 2 3 4 5 6    1 2 3 4 5 6    1 2 3 4 5 6    1 2 3 4 5 6

*When the sharp sign is at the beginning of the tune, you play all the Fs as F sharp.*

*So all the Fs in this tune are F sharp.*

The sign is on the top line of the staff because the note on this line is also called F.

F♯

# The note ladder

On the right is a note ladder. It shows all the notes you can learn to play in this book. The higher they are on the ladder, the higher the notes sound.

## Notes with the same name

Some notes have the same letter name as others. This is because they are higher or lower versions of the same note.

Which pairs of notes do not have sharp notes between them?

This C is a higher version of the C at the bottom of the ladder.

The notes in red circles are ones you can already play.

How many different notes are there?

You will learn the notes in the blue circles later in the book.

Find out the answers on page 63.

## Playing high C sharp

Hold your recorder as if you are going to play A. Now remove your left thumb.

Blow carefully as this note can easily sound out of tune.

Remember to support your recorder with your right thumb.

C' sharp is written in the third space up on the staff.

Play these measures to get used to playing the new note.

# Playing high D

Hold your recorder as if you are going to play C sharp. Then remove your first finger.

This is a higher version of the D you learned on page 18.

Play the measures below.

Listen to how similar low D and high D sound.

Can you hear that C' sharp is in between C' and D'.

High D is written on the fourth line up on the staff.

## Hot cross buns

## Royal recorders

King Henry VII of England had several recorder players in his court.

In the late fifteenth century, the recorder was one of the most popular instruments in Europe.

They could choose from up to sixteen recorders, all of different sizes.

# Tunes to play

On these two pages there are some tunes for you to play. They will help you to practice what you have learned in the book so far.

## Au *clair de la lune*

## German song

# A tune for one or two players

The tune below is called a round. You can either play it by yourself, or with someone else who plays the recorder. If you want to play it with someone else, it will help if you both practice by yourselves first.

## Folk round

## When the saints go marchin' in

# Playing a scale

A scale is made up of eight notes, played one after the other. It begins and ends on notes with the same letter name. There are several different types of scales. You can learn about the D major scale below.

The word scale comes from the Italian word *scala*, which means ladder.

Imagine that playing a scale is like climbing up or down part of the note ladder on page 24.

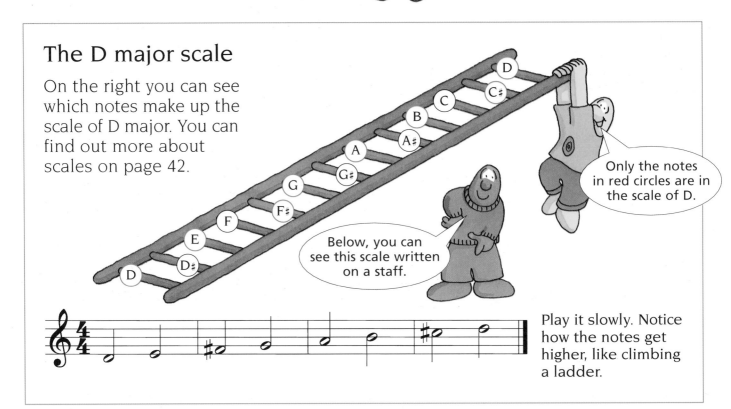

## The D major scale

On the right you can see which notes make up the scale of D major. You can find out more about scales on page 42.

Only the notes in red circles are in the scale of D.

Below, you can see this scale written on a staff.

Play it slowly. Notice how the notes get higher, like climbing a ladder.

## Distances between notes

The distance between two notes is called an interval. The interval between two notes with the same letter name, such as the two Ds in the D major scale, is called an octave.

This is an octave.

These notes are a semitone apart.

The smallest interval is a semitone. On the note ladder on the right, there is a semitone between any notes which are next to each other, such as F sharp and G.

The interval between notes which are two steps apart on the ladder is called a tone (see right). For example, the interval between D and E is a tone.

These notes are a tone apart.

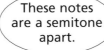

# Writing the sharps at the beginning

The D major scale can be written with the sharp signs next to the treble clef. There are two sharps in the scale of D: F sharp and C sharp. Sharp or flat signs written here are called the key signature.

This is the key signature for music based on the D major scale.

This tune is said to be in the key of D, because it is based around the scale of D major.

Remember to play all the Fs as F sharps...

...and all the Cs as C sharps.

## Can-Can

*Offenbach*

# Playing high E

Play a low E, the note you learned on page 16. Then move your left thumb a little, so you uncover a small part of the thumb hole.

When you only cover part of a hole, it is called a pinched hole.

It may be more difficult if your thumbnail is very long.

Make sure you only uncover a small part of the hole.

E'

Practice playing low E and high E, one after the other.

# Musical instructions

You can make music sound more interesting by playing notes in different ways. You can play notes loudly or quietly, smoothly or jerkily. Over the next few pages, you can find out some words and symbols which tell you how to play.

## Playing smooth notes

The Italian word for smoothly is *legato* (pronounced "le-gah-toe"). To play music *legato*, hold each note for as long as possible before gently tonguing the next note.

## Playing separate notes

A dot above or below a note tells you to play each note separately. This makes the music sound jerky. The Italian word for this is *staccato* ("sta-cah-toe").

The words and symbols which tell you how to play music are in Italian.

This is because music was first printed in Italy.

Don't stop blowing between notes!

*legato*

The word *legato* is written underneath the staff.

There are more Italian words on page 40.

Lullabies are often played *legato*.

To play *staccato* notes, say "tut" instead of "ta".

This makes your tongue stop the note as well as start it.

Don't mix up *staccato* notes with dotted notes (see page 15).

Try not to speed up. Always count carefully to keep a steady beat.

# Slurred notes

Notes on different lines or spaces with a curved line underneath them are called slurred notes. To play them, only tongue the first note, then change the fingering without tonguing again.

Find out on page 63.

# Playing loudly and quietly

As well as words that tell you how to play, there are other Italian words that tell you how loudly or quietly to play.

## Quiet music

There are three terms to tell you how quietly to play the music.

## Loud music

There are also three terms to tell you how loudly to play the music.

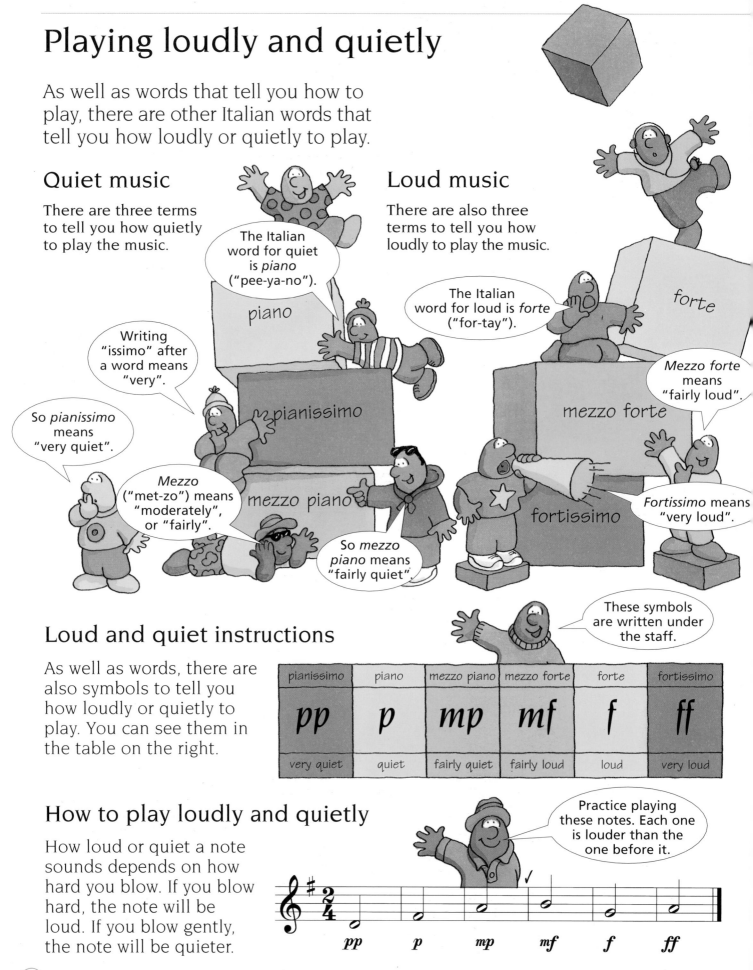

## Loud and quiet instructions

As well as words, there are also symbols to tell you how loudly or quietly to play. You can see them in the table on the right.

| pianissimo | piano | mezzo piano | mezzo forte | forte | fortissimo |
|---|---|---|---|---|---|
| **pp** | **p** | **mp** | **mf** | **f** | **ff** |
| very quiet | quiet | fairly quiet | fairly loud | loud | very loud |

## How to play loudly and quietly

How loud or quiet a note sounds depends on how hard you blow. If you blow hard, the note will be loud. If you blow gently, the note will be quieter.

# Very short notes

Sometimes in music there are very short notes, called sixteenth notes. A sixteenth note lasts for half an eighth beat.

Sixteenth notes can be joined together by two lines.

It can be hard to tongue sixteenth notes.

An eighth note is worth two sixteenth notes.

Sixteenth note tails can be joined to eighth note tails.

There are four sixteenth notes in one quarter beat.

ta-ta  ta-ga-ta-ga

You may find it easier to say "ta-ga-ta-ga" as you play them, instead of "ta-ta-ta-ta".

## The keeper

ta  ta-ga  ta  ta-ga

ta - ga ta - ga     ta  ta - ga

It may help to clap the rhythm before starting to play.

## Playing low C

Put your fingers down as if you are playing D, then put your right-hand little finger over the two small holes on the foot joint.

Low C is written below the staff on a special line called a ledger line.

This is the lowest note you can play on a soprano recorder.

Make sure you cover both small holes.

Blow very gently. It is easy to squeak when you are playing this note.

Ledger lines are used for notes which are above or below the staff.

C

On some recorders you can twist the foot joint to make it easier to reach these holes.

Practice this measure until you are used to the fingering.

# Natural notes

A natural note is any note which is not a sharp or a flat. You can find out more about flat notes on page 36.

*This is a natural sign.*

*Without the natural sign, this note would be C sharp.*

## Natural signs

A natural sign cancels the effect of a sharp or flat sign earlier in the measure.

A natural sign also cancels the effect of any sharps or flats in the key signature.

*C sharp*  *C natural*

*Key signature*  *F sharp*  *F natural*

*A natural sign affects all the notes after it in the measure on the same line or space...*

*...so this note is F natural, too.*

*This note is F sharp, because it is in the next measure.*

## Playing low F

Put your fingers down as if you are going to play low C. Then lift your right-hand middle finger. This note is F.

*Keep your first and third right-hand fingers down all the way through this measure.*

*Make sure you cover both small holes with your little finger.*

*Can you hear how F sharp is between F and G?*

*F is written in the bottom space on the staff.*

F

You might find the fingering for F a little awkward at first.

Practice these measures to help you get used to it.

# The C major scale

Below, you can see the notes in the C major scale. Practice this scale until you can play it smoothly.

There are no sharps in this scale, so there is no key signature for tunes in the key of C major.

Now you know two scales...

...C major and D major.

Practice these scales each time you play your recorder.

## Tunes to play

This tune will help you to practice the scale of C major.

### Unto us a child is born

Piae Cantiones 1582

### Entry of the clowns

# More in-between notes

On page 22 you found out about sharps. There is another kind of in-between note called a flat.

## Flat notes

A flat note is a semitone lower than the note it takes its name from. Each in-between note has two names, a sharp and a flat one. For example, F sharp can also be called G flat.

Even though they are the same note, they are written in different places on the staff.

## Playing B flat

Play G on your recorder. Then lift your left-hand middle finger and put down your right-hand first finger. This is B flat.

This is a flat sign.

This note can be called F sharp or G flat.

Each step is a semitone apart.

You can find out why in-between notes have two names on page 42.

This note is F sharp.

This note is G flat.

Can you figure out the two names for the note in between A and B?

Find out the answer on page 63.

Remember to look at the key signature.

All of the B's below are B flats.

The note B flat is written on the middle line of the staff.

This note can be called B flat or A sharp.

Practice the measures above until you can play them smoothly.

# Getting louder and quieter

There are Italian words and symbols that tell you to get louder or quieter. *Crescendo* (cre-shen-doe) means "get gradually louder", and *diminuendo* (di-min-you-en-doe) means "get gradually quieter".

## Henry VIII's recorders

Henry VIII of England (1491-1547) loved the recorder. When he died, he left a collection of 76 recorders, including a box of eight recorders made from ivory (elephant tusks).

## All *through the night*

Before you start, check the music for symbols telling you how loudly or quietly to play.

B♭

# Tunes to play

On these two pages there are some tunes for you to play.

## The holly and the ivy

## I saw three ships

# My Bonnie lies over the ocean

## Rachel's round

This tune is another round, like the one on page 27. You can play it with a friend, if you like.

# More musical instructions

On these two pages you can find out about more Italian words and symbols.

## Playing quickly or slowly

As well as words that tell you how loudly or quietly to play, there are also words that tell you how quickly or slowly to play. These words are written above the staff, at the beginning of the music.

The Italian word for fast is *allegro* (a-leg-roe).

A folk dance might be played *allegro*.

The Italian word for slowly is *lento* (len-toe).

A romantic tune might be played *lento*.

The word for a speed between *allegro* and *lento* is *andante* (an-dan-tay).

*Andante* means "at a walking pace".

The speed of a tune is known as its tempo. If a tune has a fast tempo, it is played quickly.

## Playing high F and high F sharp

Put your fingers down as if you are going to play high E. Then lift your right-hand middle finger and put down your right-hand third finger. This is high F.

Now lift your right-hand first and third fingers, and put down your second finger. This is high F sharp.

If the note is an F sharp, it has a sharp sign before the note, or in the key signature.

High F and high F sharp are both written on the top line of the staff.

F'/F#'

Practice playing these measures a few times to get used to the notes.

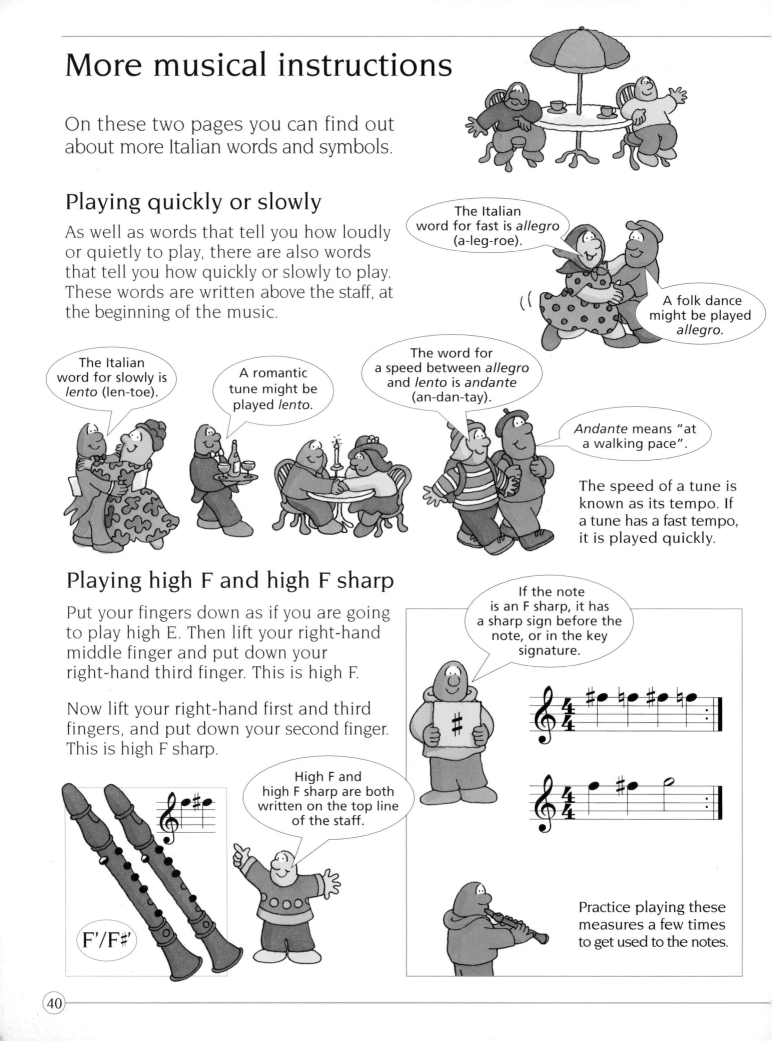

# Getting gradually slower

The word *ritardando* (rit-ah-dan-doe) tells you to get gradually slower. It is often shortened to *rit*.

*rit.*     *a tempo*

**When you see** the word *ritardando* in the middle of a tune, it is often followed by *a tempo*.

**The tempo slows** down, just like a train slows down as it pulls into a station.

*A tempo* tells you to return to the speed you were playing at before.

**The word** *ritardando*, or *rit.*, is written under the staff.

# D. C. al Fine

D. C. *al Fine* stands for *Da Capo al Fine*. This tells you to go back to the beginning of the piece and play the music again until you reach the word *Fine* (fee-nay). Then stop playing.

**Go back to** the beginning and start again.

**The second** time through, stop when you reach the word *Fine*.

*Fine*     *D.C. al Fine*

*mf*

# The pause sign

A pause sign tells you to hold the note for a little bit longer than usual.

You often see pause signs at the end of a tune, or at the end of a *ritardando* section.

# The spy

Look out for the Italian words in this tune before you start to play.

**Remember** to play this tune slowly.

Lento

*p*

1.    2.    *Fine*

$<$ *f* $>$ *p*     *ff*

*D.C. al Fine*

F'
F#'

# More about scales

So far you have learned to play the scales of D major (on page 28) and C major (on page 35). On these two pages you can find out how to figure out which notes are in other major scales.

## Figuring out the notes in a scale

Every major scale has eight notes. On the right you can see the intervals between each of the notes.

This ladder shows the notes in a C major scale.

This ladder shows the notes in a D major scale.

A yellow block shows an interval of a tone.

A red block shows an interval of a semitone.

The pattern of tones and semitones is the same for each scale.

You can use this pattern to figure out the notes in other major scales.

C
B
A
G
F
E
D
C

semitone
tone
tone
tone
semitone
tone
tone

D
C♯
B
A
G
F♯
E
D

## The scale of F major

Following the steps below, try to figure out the notes in the F major scale.

① Draw a ladder thirteen steps high on a piece of paper.

② Write the letter F on the bottom step and the top step.

Use the big note ladder on page 24 to help you.

③ Look at the pattern of intervals in the scales above.

④ The second note up is a tone higher than F. This note is G, so now write G on your note ladder.

Write the note two steps up for a tone...

⑤ Figure out the next note in the same way. This note is A, so write this on your ladder above the G.

...and one step up for a semitone.

⑥ The next note is a semitone up. In F major, it is called B flat because each note must be on a new line or space.

⑦ Continue until you have eight notes on the ladder. You can check to see if you have the right notes on the next page.

# The key of F major

A scale can have sharps or flats in the key signature, but never both. Tunes in the key of F major have a B flat in the key signature.

It is never called A sharp in the F major scale.

Otherwise there would be two notes on the second space up...

This note is called B flat.

...and no note on the middle line.

Practice this scale until you can play it without any mistakes.

# Playing high G

Put your fingers down as if you are playing high F sharp. Then lift your right-hand middle finger. This is high G.

High G is written in the space above the staff.

This is the highest note in this book.

G'

There are higher notes, but they are not played very often.

*Gee up!*

Practice this tune to help you get used to the new note.

# The scale of G major

Try to figure out the scale of G major, following the same steps that you used for F major.

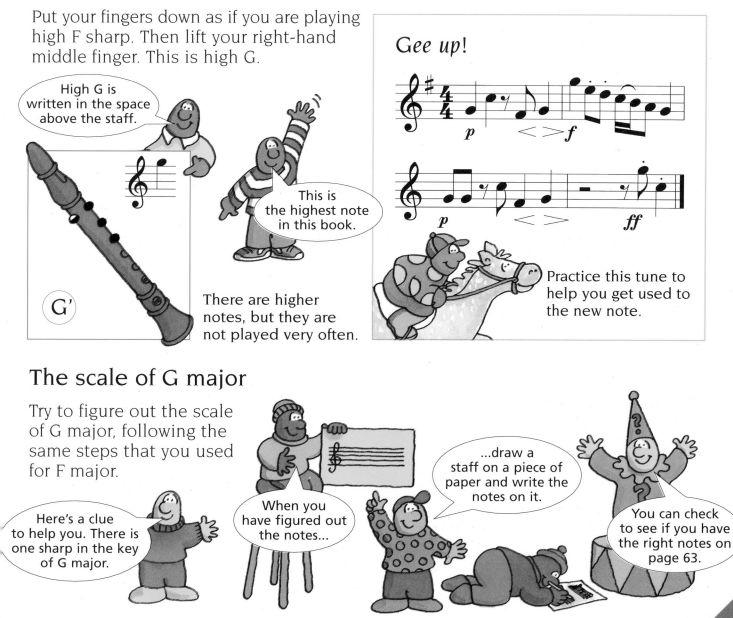

Here's a clue to help you. There is one sharp in the key of G major.

When you have figured out the notes...

...draw a staff on a piece of paper and write the notes on it.

You can check to see if you have the right notes on page 63.

# More notes to play

There are four new notes below. When you can play them, you will be able to play every note on the big note ladder on page 24.

## Playing low C sharp

Play a low C, then slide your little finger very slowly off the double hole until the smaller of the two holes is uncovered.

This note can also be called D flat.

Make sure you uncover this hole completely.

C#

Practice the measure on the left to get used to the fingering.

## Playing low D sharp

Play low D, then slide your right-hand third finger off the double hole until the smaller of the two holes is uncovered.

This note can also be called low E flat.

Make sure you uncover this hole completely.

D#

The measure on the left will help you to practice the fingering.

## Playing low G sharp

Put your fingers down as if you are going to play low D sharp. Now remove your left-hand third finger.

This note can also be called A flat.

The fingering for this note is fairly difficult.

G#

Practice this measure until you can play the notes smoothly.

## Playing high D sharp

Put your fingers down as if you are going to play low D. Now remove your left-hand thumb and first finger.

This note can also be called high E flat.

D#'

Play this measure a few times to get used to the notes.

# Playing tips

You have now learned enough to play all the tunes in this book. On this page there are some extra tips to help you play them well.

## Before you play

Always make a few simple checks before you start to play a tune.

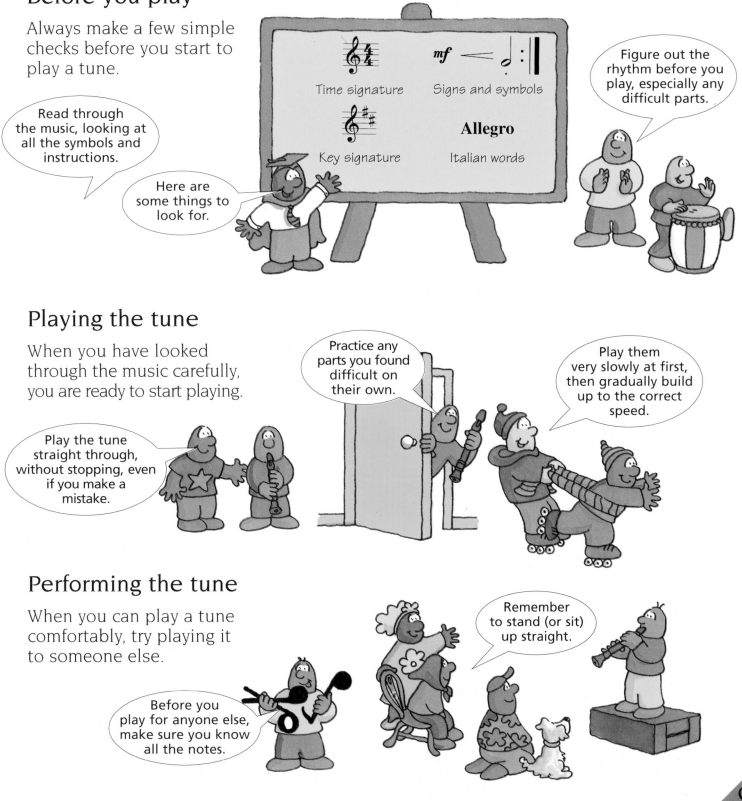

Read through the music, looking at all the symbols and instructions.

Here are some things to look for.

Time signature

Signs and symbols

Key signature

*Allegro*

Italian words

Figure out the rhythm before you play, especially any difficult parts.

## Playing the tune

When you have looked through the music carefully, you are ready to start playing.

Practice any parts you found difficult on their own.

Play them very slowly at first, then gradually build up to the correct speed.

Play the tune straight through, without stopping, even if you make a mistake.

## Performing the tune

When you can play a tune comfortably, try playing it to someone else.

Remember to stand (or sit) up straight.

Before you play for anyone else, make sure you know all the notes.

G♯
D♯'
D♯  C♯'

# More tunes to play

On the next few pages there are lots of tunes for you to play and perform. Look at the tips on page 45 if you need any help.

## Red river valley

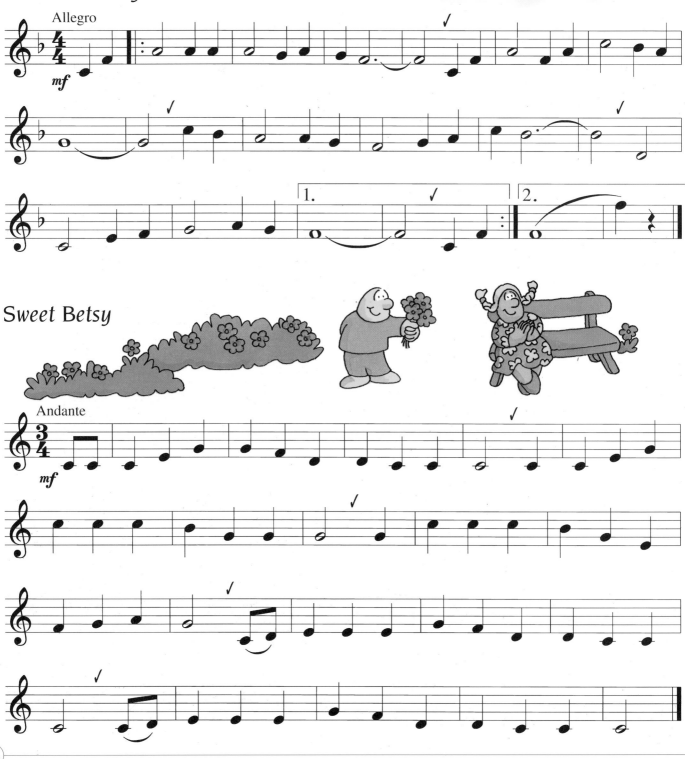

## Sweet Betsy

# Tit willow

Sullivan

# Scarborough fair

48

# When Johnny comes marching home

The Lincolnshire poacher

# Pat-a-pan

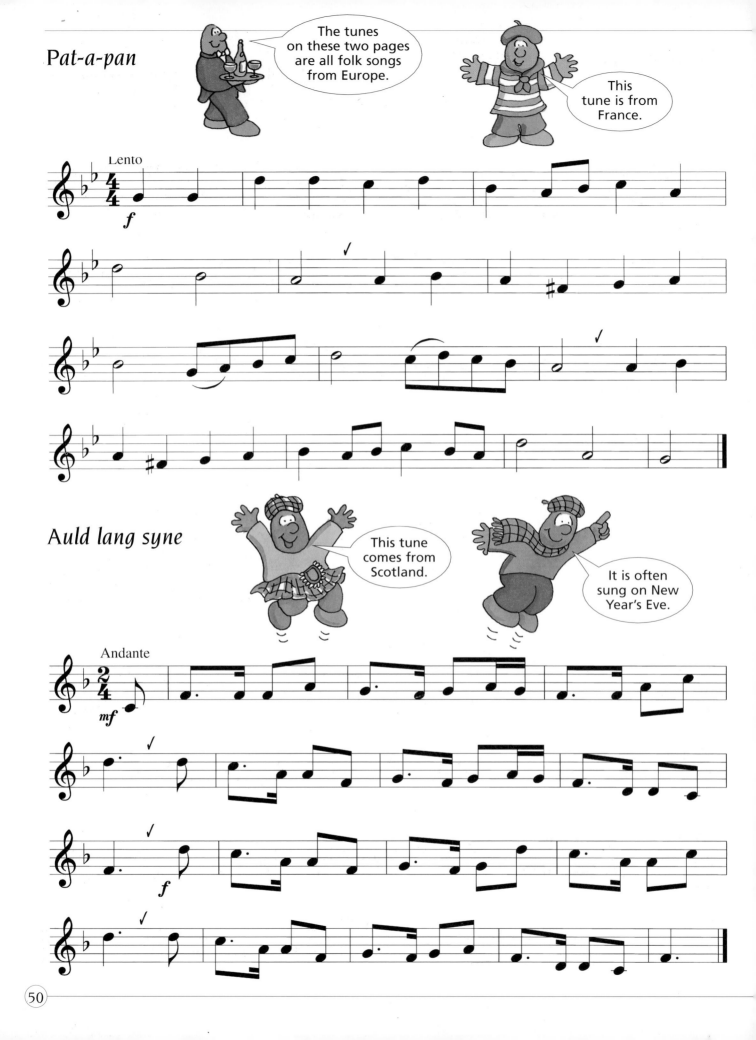

# Auld lang syne

# Rocking song

# Lord of all hopefulness

# Morning (from "Peer Gynt")

Grieg

# The Blue Danube

Strauss

# From the New World

Dvořák

## Arietta

Mozart

## Good King Wenceslas

The next four tunes are all Christmas carols.

Piae Cantiones 1582

## Hark! The herald angels sing

Mendelssohn

# Tunes for two players

On these two pages there are some tunes for you to play with a friend. Tunes for two people are called duets. There is a separate staff for each player.

Both players need to start at exactly the same time. To help you to do this, decide how fast you want to play, then count a measure together before you start.

## *What shall we do with the drunken sailor*

# Mango walk

# Tunes for recorder and piano

You can play the next two tunes on your own, or with a piano. The top staff is the recorder part and the bottom two staffs are the piano part.

## Greensleeves

# Pastime with good company

King Henry VIII

# The recorder family

There are lots of different types of recorders. The four most common ones are the sopranino, soprano, alto and tenor recorders.

A sopranino recorder

A soprano recorder

An alto recorder

A tenor recorder

*This recorder has a key at the bottom to cover the lowest hole...*

*...and a support on the back for your right thumb.*

This is the smallest of the four most common recorders. It is about 24cm (9.5in) long. It plays higher notes than the soprano recorder.

The most common recorder is called the soprano. It is also the cheapest. The tunes in this book are for the soprano recorder.

This recorder is about 48cm (19in) long. It plays lower notes than the soprano recorder and it makes a very rich sound.

At 64cm (25in), this is the longest of these recorders. The notes it plays are an octave lower than the notes on a soprano recorder.

## Rarer recorders

There are several other types of recorders which are not seen very often.

The largest is a sub-contra bass recorder. It is over 3m (10ft) high and costs more than 300 times as much as this book.

*You have to blow through a tube which is nearly 2m (6½ft) long.*

*It has lots of keys to cover the holes because they are so far apart.*

*This recorder has to rest on the floor on a special stand.*

The smallest is a garklein recorder. It is only about 12cm (4.75in) long. This is about as long as the head-joint on a soprano recorder.

*A garklein recorder is easier to play if you have small hands...*

*...because the holes are so close together.*

# Buying a soprano recorder

A soprano recorder is one of the cheapest musical instruments you can buy. Below there is a table to show you some well-known makes.

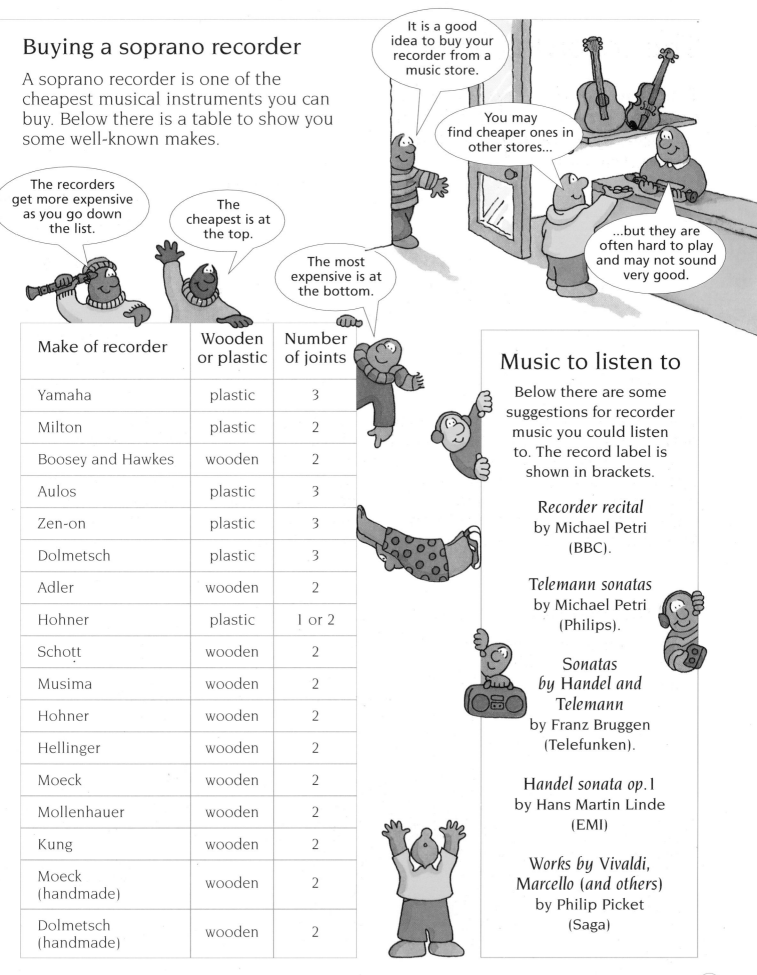

| Make of recorder | Wooden or plastic | Number of joints |
|---|---|---|
| Yamaha | plastic | 3 |
| Milton | plastic | 2 |
| Boosey and Hawkes | wooden | 2 |
| Aulos | plastic | 3 |
| Zen-on | plastic | 3 |
| Dolmetsch | plastic | 3 |
| Adler | wooden | 2 |
| Hohner | plastic | 1 or 2 |
| Schott | wooden | 2 |
| Musima | wooden | 2 |
| Hohner | wooden | 2 |
| Hellinger | wooden | 2 |
| Moeck | wooden | 2 |
| Mollenhauer | wooden | 2 |
| Kung | wooden | 2 |
| Moeck (handmade) | wooden | 2 |
| Dolmetsch (handmade) | wooden | 2 |

## Music to listen to

Below there are some suggestions for recorder music you could listen to. The record label is shown in brackets.

*Recorder recital*
by Michael Petri
(BBC).

*Telemann sonatas*
by Michael Petri
(Philips).

*Sonatas by Handel and Telemann*
by Franz Bruggen
(Telefunken).

*Handel sonata op.1*
by Hans Martin Linde
(EMI)

*Works by Vivaldi, Marcello (and others)*
by Philip Picket
(Saga)

# Music help

The list below explains the Italian words used in this book, as well as some other words that may be unfamiliar.

| | |
|---|---|
| A *tempo* | Play the music at the original speed. |
| *Allegro* | Play the music fast. |
| *Andante* | Play the music at a walking pace. |
| *Crescendo* | Get gradually louder. |
| *Da capo al Fine* | Go back to the beginning and play the music again until you reach the word *Fine*. |
| *Diminuendo* | Get gradually quieter. |
| Duet | A piece of music for two players. |
| *Fine* | The end of the music (see *Da capo al Fine*). |
| *Forte* | Play the music loudly. |
| *Fortissimo* | Play very loudly. |
| Interval | The distance between two notes. |
| Key | The letter name of the scale upon which the music is based. |
| Key signature | Sharps or flats written at the beginning of the music. |

| | |
|---|---|
| Ledger line | Extra lines for notes that are too high or low to fit on the staff. |
| *Legato* | Play very smoothly. |
| *Lento* | Play the music slowly. |
| *Mezzo forte* | Play fairly loudly. |
| *Mezzo piano* | Play fairly quietly. |
| Octave | The interval between two notes with the same letter name. |
| *Piano* | Play the music quietly. |
| *Pianissimo* | Play very quietly. |
| *Ritardando* | Get gradually slower. |
| Round | A tune which can be played by several players, each starting at a different time. |
| Scale | A series of eight notes which have a set pattern of intervals between them. The first and last notes are an octave apart. |
| Semitone | The smallest interval between two notes, for example F and F sharp. |

| | | | |
|---|---|---|---|
| Slur | A line which links two or more notes at different places on the staff. Only the first note should be tongued. | Tie | A line which links two notes on the same line or space. Add the lengths of the notes together. |
| *Staccato* | Shown by a dot above or below a note. *Staccato* notes should be short and spiky. | Tone | An interval of two semitones, for example between F and G. |
| *Tempo* | The speed of the music. | | |

## Answers

**Page 11** There are four measures in this tune, with four beats in each measure.

**Page 12** A whole note is worth two half beats.

**Page 18** The tied notes on the left are worth seven quarter beats. The tied notes on the right are worth five quarter beats.

**Page 21** The orders in which you would play these measures are:

1 2 3 4  5 6 5 6
1 2 1 2  3 4 5 5
1 2 3 1 2 3  4 5 4 5

**Page 24** The notes E and F and the notes B and C do not have sharp notes between them. There are twenty different notes on the note ladder.

**Page 31** *Legato* notes are gently tongued, but you only tongue the first note in a group of slurred notes.

**Page 36** The two names for the note in between A and B are A sharp and B flat.

**Page 43** This is the scale of G major. There is an F sharp in the key signature.

# Index

## Notes

| | | | |
|---|---|---|---|
| B - 8 | C' - 21 | C - 33 | G' - 43 |
| A - 12 | F♯ - 22 | F - 34 | C♯ - 44 |
| G - 14 | C♯ - 24 | B♭ - 36 | D♯ - 44 |
| E - 16 | D' - 25 | F' - 40 | D♯' - 44 |
| D - 18 | E' - 29 | F♯' - 40 | G♯ - 44 |

First published in 1986 by Usborne Publishing Ltd, Usborne House, 83-85 Saffron Hill, London EC1N 8RT. Copyright © 1997, 1991, 1986 Usborne Publishing Ltd. The name Usborne and the devices are Trade Marks of Usborne Publishing Ltd. All rights reserved. No part of this publication may be reproduced, stored in a retrieval system or transmitted in any form or by any means, electronic, mechanical, photocopying, recording or otherwise, without the prior permission of the publisher. Printed in Great Britain.
This edition first published in America, August 1997. AE.